The
First Breath

William Lucas Hollingsworth

ISBN

Hardcover: 978-1-969844-11-9

Paperback: 978-1-969844-10-2

About the Author

My name is William Lucas Hollingsworth. I go by William at school, and my mom calls me Lucas. I am currently in the 11th grade at York Comprehensive High School in York, SC it's a huge school that looks like a college in a small country town. It's perfect for my family. My mom and dad split years ago, and my dad has me and my brother every other weekend. It's just me and my ten-year-old brother, Jake or Jacob, when my mom is mad at him. Down at my dad's house in Chester, we have his wife, Hannah, and her three kids. I love my mom and dad a lot and appreciate everything they do for me and help me become the person I am becoming. After I graduate, I plan to attend college to become a Registered Nurse. I also have a passion for writing, and my imagination is evident in the book I've written. My hobbies include watching TV, Netflix, and chill, as well as building with Legos. My brother and I have a building out back that has Legos galore. I bet we have over 200 Legos in that building, and we're still getting more!

Table of Contents

Chapter 1:
Game Plan

It was a dusky day in mid-October. My best friend, Auron, and I sat at our desks in school while our teacher, Miss Ackle, lectured us on geometry and other subjects. However, we weren't paying attention.

After class, as we walked home, and during that, something extraordinary happened: a giant hole opened in the sky, and a man dressed in a black robe emerged. Suddenly, the sky turned dark. He announced, "My name is Zoltor, and I have come to bring about the end of this planet."

At that moment, a massive dragon appeared, with black and orange scales. Alarmed, Auron and I ran to his house. When we got there, we saw Auron's parents, but suddenly, a blast struck the house, and in an instant, his home and family were gone. The world plunged into chaos, and in confusion, Auron and I sprinted away.

As we ran, I caught a glimpse of my dad for the first time in twelve years, but before I could reach him, he disappeared.

Everything felt surreal and terrifying, but we couldn't give up. We rushed to the nearest grocery store to stock up on supplies.

Inside the store, we spotted Zoltor conversing with five masked figures. They were Apostles named Copon, Zindin, and Zordin.

Zoltar was one of five demonic spirits—the harbinger of doom. Auron and I overheard them discussing the Orb of

Balance, which they believed would give them the power to rule the universe.

Just then, Auron accidentally knocked something over, drawing Zoltor's attention. He lifted us both into the air and demanded to know why we were there. Auron, in a burst of defiance, spat in Zoltor's face, provoking him to throw Auron aside.

In retaliation, I kicked Zoltor in the face, and we both ran for our lives as he chased us. Miraculously, my eyes turned red, and when Zoltor looked at me, I found myself lifting a car with no hands and throwing it at him. He crashed to the ground, and that's when I blacked out.

When I regained consciousness, I found myself back in my old house. There, I saw Ana, a girl from school I had a crush on since fifth grade.

She asked if I was okay, and I replied, "Yeah." Her blonde hair was tied up in a ponytail with pink highlights, and her hazel eyes were filled with concern. She helped me to my feet, and just then, Auron rushed over, hugged me tightly, and asked, "What just happened?" I responded, "I don't even know." I felt a surge of energy within me.

Although it made no sense, because none of my family had ever possessed any powers. I knew that I had them. However, that wasn't our primary concern. We needed to retrieve the Orb of Balance from Zoltor before he could destroy the universe.

Auron asked me what we should do, and I remembered that there was a bookshelf in the basement that might hold answers. We headed down to the basement, where I found a book titled "Family Secrets." Opening the book, I was shocked to see a picture of my dad using his power of air to control the weather alongside an image of Zoltor. I thought to myself, why is he in my family book?

Turning around, I was shocked to see my deceased mother standing in front of me. She told me that to stop Zoltor, I would need the Orb of Balance, which was hidden deep in the jungles of Peru.

Returning to reality, I informed Ana and Auron about the location of the Orb. Auron expressed concern, saying we couldn't go to Peru because the planes were grounded, and if Zoltor saw us, we would be doomed. I reassured him that Zoltor would miss us. We hopped into the car and drove to the airport, utterly unaware that Zoltor had a spy watching us.

Upon arriving at the airport, I saw my mom one last time. She warned me to be careful because there was a spy within our group. She explained that the Orb of Balance was a relic from millions of years ago and that Zoltor had been trying to obtain it for years, ever since my dad humiliated him at the Grand Council.

I asked her what had happened, and she explained that my dad made a comment that ruined Zoltor, ultimately leading to her death. Zoltor had attempted to blast my dad but ended up hitting me instead, which caused Council to banish Zoltor to the underworld forever.

If Zoltor were to obtain the Orb of Balance, he could destroy everything and take over the universe. However, it wasn't the only thing he needed. I asked my mom what else he required, and she revealed that he needed my soul energy. Confused, I questioned why he needed that. She explained that this was how I had to start, as I was trying to understand my powers.

Before I could ask her why his picture was in the photo book, she disappeared. Then I passed out and woke up halfway to Peru. Looking out the window, I saw the orange and black dragon return, and suddenly, the plane crashed. I remembered there was a traitor among us and asked Ana and Auron who it was, but nobody answered. Then, they both vanished. That's when Zoltar appeared and said, "You want to know why I'm in the picture book, right?"

I asked him how he knew about it, and he replied, "Because I am your uncle." Then he disappeared again.

I saw Auron and Ana looking terrified, just like the orange and black dragon. At that moment, I charged up with the color red and created a sword out of thin air. I cut off all three heads of the dragon, and I passed out again.

When I woke up again, we were in Peru. I asked, "Where is everyone?" The markets were deserted, and all the houses were in shambles, but we kept going and walked into the jungle.

There, we met a boy named Carlos; he was the only one who survived the attack by the Leviathan on his village. He turned to the jungle. Auron, Ana, and I asked him if he needed help, and he said, "Yeah." I then asked if he could guide us to the center of the jungle.

He wondered why, and I said, "Because I am trying to stop this madness." He replied, "Follow me," and we ventured deeper into the jungle. I asked him why he didn't leave Peru. He said, "Because I hoped that someone would fix my village." Suddenly, I saw my mother again and asked her why she hadn't told me that Zoltor was my uncle. She replied, "Because if you knew, he would find out where you were." I inquired how he got into the picture book, and she explained that the book was created before the Grand Council meeting.

Then, I returned to the real world and kept wondering about the identity of the traitor. We finally made it to the middle of the jungle, and Carlos asked why I needed to come here.

At that moment, I powered up, punched a hole straight through the ground, and jumped down. Below, we found ourselves in an ancient temple. As we explored the old temple, I saw my mom going through ancient scrolls. I called out, "Mom," and she turned around, exclaiming, "Surprise!"

Chapter 2:
Plot Twist and Twist and Twist

I said to myself, "I thought she died." She even mentioned that Zoltor killed her during the Grand Council meeting. Suddenly, she approached me and explained that she wanted to tell me she was alive, but if she did, Zoltor would come after her.

I tell her that I don't have time for this and ask her where the Orb of Balance is. She tells me that it's on the other side of Peru. Frustrated, I yelled at her, asking why she wanted me to come here.

Then, Auron, Ana, and I make our way to the other side of the island, where we encounter Zoltor. I charge up and fight him. During the battle, he asks if I knew there was a traitor. I told him my mom said so. He responds, "Wait, your mom is alive? Oh, the fight will be fun!" He then pulls out his giant scythe and says, "Let's duel."

Suddenly, I see Auron come up behind me. He apologizes and stabs me with the dagger I gave him. I pass out and wake up in the cavern of orbs. I see Zoltor holding the Orb of Balance. Breaking free from the ropes, I grab Ana and the Orb of Balance, then jump from the cliff into the ocean.

We start to drown, but then my water powers activate, allowing us to dive deep into the sea. We arrive in the underwater kingdom, and I help Ana up. I asked her if she knew he was a traitor. She responds that she didn't, and I sat down and cried from the sting of betrayal.

The Sea King approaches and helps me up. He asks what's wrong and says, "My friend, he betrayed me."

Meanwhile, in the cavern of orbs, Zoltor is furious that the Orb of Balance is gone. Auron tells him to calm down, but Zoltor refuses and declares that he must destroy me. He yells that without the Orb, he can't fix all the problems he caused.

Auron asks how destroying me will solve those problems, and Zoltor replies that it can reverse time, giving him the chance to kill my mother and father at the same time and then take down the Grand Council.

I tell the Sea King I need to see my mother. He takes me to her, and I ask why she kept this hidden. She replies, "To protect you." I ask her how to stop Zoltor, and she reveals that the only way is to collect the 14 Orbs of Power. I ask her what those are, and she explains they are four ultimate time cores that can alter the fabric of time according to someone's wish.

"Each core is hidden in a different realm, guarded by ancient beings who will test your worthiness," she continues, her voice steady but laced with urgency.

"You must gather all fourteen Orbs and unite them, or Zoltor will plunge our world into chaos." With them, I can save my parents and stop Zoltor.

Zoltor then tells Auron that he used to be good, but the Grand Council messed with his lifeline, cutting both good and bad aspects from him.

I then ask my mom where to find the 14 Orbs of Power. She lists their locations: one in the Parallel Nation, one in the Abyss Yonder, one in the Undying Isles, one in the Ivory Realms, one in the Ever Isles, one in the Wild Land, one in the Hallow Vale, one in Storm Lake, one in the Peaceful Vale, one in Onyx Mines, one in the Perfect Nation, one in the Immortal Moon, one in the Love Valley, and finally one in the Faint Sanctuary.

My mom asks if she can come along, and I agree, but tell her not to mess anything up. She promises she won't. I then ask her how we can get to the Parallel Nation, and she explains that if we reach the launchpad, we can make it there.

As we make our way back through the jungle, we find Carlos and ask if he wants to join us. He agrees, and I promise to fix everything. We start walking toward the launchpad when we encounter Zoltor and Auron again.

When Zoltor sees my mom, he questions how she is still alive. I tell him to leave her alone, and he suggests that I'm holding too many burdens and need to let go. Angered, I punch him in the face, and a battle ensues.

Zoltor tells me I need to get my act together. In a moment of rage, I kick him off the cliff, and he disappears. I use my powers to knock Auron unconscious. When Auron wakes up, I ask him what Zoltor told him.

He explains that the Grand Council tricked Zoltor and severed his connection to both goodness and evil. He then apologizes to me but suddenly tries to stab me. I kick him away and can finally see the launchpad in the distance.

Just then, a new threat emerges, which is a two-headed goblin named Ta-ta. He grabs Ana and Carlos, and I yell at Auron to help. Together with my mom, we work to rescue Carlos and Ana. I hold a stick and hit the goblin, but he shoots fire at me. As I charge up my powers, I feel them being drained. I realize Auron is stealing my soul energy, and then he reveals his proper form as Zordin. I come to the horrifying realization that my real friend, Auron, is still alive and that when we encountered Zoltor at the grocery store, Zordin and Auron had switched places.

My faithful friend is out there, but where? Suddenly, I pass out and wake up near the launchpad. The only thing left is to navigate the water caverns ahead. However, as we enter, the cavern begins to flood, and I start to drown. Everyone else makes it out, but I die.

I then find myself before the Grand Council, who revive me. I take a deep breath, and Ana encourages me, saying, "Come on, we are almost there!" Finally, we arrive at the launchpad, and in the distance, among the trees, I spot my dad. But Zoltor isn't going to let us leave without causing trouble.

Suddenly, the Leviathan attacks the launchpad, triggering PTSD in Carlos from when the Leviathan destroyed his village. At that moment, he realizes he has powers just like mine and conjures fire, ultimately burning the Leviathan's head off. Zoltor suddenly appears, holding Auron hostage. He threatens, "If you get into that launch shuttle, I will kill him right here, right now."

Carlos and I prepare to fight Zoltor, but before we can land a hit, the sky turns black, and five demonic spirits emerge: Apostles, Copon, Zindin, and Zordin. They engage us in battle, and Ana jumps in to help fight as well. As Zoltor approaches my mother, he asks, "How are you still alive?" In response, she kicks him hard and retorts, "Guess you didn't finish me off." The two of them begin to fight, and during the chaos, she yells at me to apologize for being a bad mother. In a shocking turn of events, she takes her knife and stabs Zoltor first through his back, then plunges it into her stomach. Zoltor pretends to die but then pushes her off the cliff and heals himself.

Meanwhile, Carlos, Ana, Auron, and I climb into the launch shuttle. I press the button to launch it, and as we take off, I watch my mother and father disappear. In an instant, I see Earth explode into tiny pieces.

Chapter 3:
A Heck of a Goose Chase

We arrive at the Parallel Nation and meet a person named Zee-Zee, who introduces herself as the leader of this realm. She guides us to a maze of mirrors and explains that what we're looking for is hidden within one of the thousands of mirrors. I think to myself, "No way," but we proceed into the maze anyway.

As we walk through, Ana accidentally bumps into one of the mirrors, causing it to shatter. To our horror, the mirror grabs her and pulls her in. Without hesitation, I jump in after her. Inside, we are confronted by our worst nightmares.

I see my parents and the Grand Council being killed by Zoltor. Ana witnesses her entire world crumbling beneath her, while Auron sees his mother and father disappointed in him for not saving them.

Zee-Zee then tells us that if we face our fears, we can escape the mirror. She explains that to overcome our nightmares, we must conquer them. Summoning my courage, I walk up to the Zoltor in my vision and defeat it. My eyes surge with red power, and then I wake up, stepping out of the broken mirror.

Next, Zee-Zee helps Ana confront her nightmare. She tells her that these nightmares are not real, allowing Ana to awaken and emerge from her mirror.

Zee-Zee then assists Auron, who tells his parents to "suck it up" and not to be disappointed in him. He, too, wakes up and exits the mirror.

Afterward, Zee-Zee guides us out of the maze and informs us that the next step to reach the Core of Integrity involves navigating winding roads and paths.

Once we arrived, I asked Zee-Zee what the Core of Integrity is. She explains that it represents the quality of being honest and having strong moral principles. I then ask if it grants this quality, and she confirms that it does. As we navigate the winding roads and paths, each of us takes a different route.

Suddenly, I encounter Zoltor, who warns me to stop or face serious consequences. Ignoring his threat, I retaliate and hit him back. Zoltor then tells me that my friends are illusions and that I will end up just like him. Looking at him, I reply, "Maybe I am." My eyes turn red, and in a sudden burst of anger, I hit Zoltor. He then disappears, allowing me to escape the winding road.

I soon see Ana and Auron making their way out as well, but Zee-Zee has not escaped. She instructs us to go on without her to Pará's Village.

Upon arriving at Pará's Village, I notice images of Zoltor everywhere. However, they are merely projections from the Pará and not real. I speak with some of the Pará, and one of them tells me that the Core of Integrity is located atop Mount. Para.

I hear Zee-Zee yelling for help, but Ana insists we should leave her behind. I argue that this is not the right thing to do, so we decide to go back and help her. Zoltar is attacking her. I kick him in the face and use my powers; my eyes turn a dark red. Then, I kick him off the cliff, and he falls into the Abyss below.

After saving Zee-Zee, we finally reach the top of the mountain and discover the Orb of Integrity. Zee-Zee picks it up and asks me if I have integrity. I reply that I do not. She then asks, "Who does?" I look at her, and she quickly says, "No, no, no, not me. I'm not the one to trust with this Orb."

I respond, "Zee-Zee, will you join our team?" She agrees, saying, "Yeah."

As we made our way back to the launch shuttle, I couldn't help but wonder if I was becoming like Zoltor. The gang and I had arrived at The Abyss Yonder, where we found ourselves in a deserted town with a population of just one person—a little boy named Todo.

When I asked him where his parents were, he told me they were stuck in a place called No Tail Lands. Curious, I inquired about what No Tail Lands were, and he explained that it was a location out in the desert. I assured him that I would help him get his parents back and asked who had taken them hostage.

He replied that it was Zoltor, and I recognized the name immediately—Zoltor, the Bringer of Doom. I told Todo to take me to his weapons, and he led us to his house. There, we went behind a bookshelf to access a hidden safe room filled with weapons. Armed and ready, we set out for No Tail Lands. When we confronted Zoltor, I noticed he had a cut on his arm and a black eye.

He stood tall and asked if I had conceded to his offer. I firmly replied no, and we engaged in a fierce battle. He taunted me, saying that if I joined him, he could bring my parents back. I shot back that he was the reason my parents were gone in the first place. He smugly confirmed this, adding that my mother had screamed as he chopped off her head.

Fueled by rage, I attacked him with all my might, but it wasn't enough. Just then, Ana, Auron, Zee-Zee, and Todo rescued their parents and dragged my unconscious body away.

We managed to return to the deserted village, and when I woke up, I asked Todo if he knew where the Bottomless Cavern was. He replied that since I saved his family, he could take me there.

As we journeyed to the cavern, Todo asked me why I sought it. I explained that the Orb of Kindness was located there. Curious about his family's situation, I wondered why Todo and his parents were the only ones left. He recounted how, when five demonic spirits attacked, they took everyone away, leaving just him and his family. I then asked how far away the Bottomless Cavern was.

As I walked ahead, I stumbled and fell into the cavern. Todo and the gang jumped in after me. Once inside, I spotted the door to the Abyss, but before I could reach it, a giant red spider descended from above, followed by five enormous snakes. The gang and I sprang into action, slicing and dicing at our attackers. In the chaos, Todo charged at one of the snakes, only to be bitten and poisoned. I rushed to save him, but it was too late; he had already passed away.

In the distance, I saw the Orb of Kindness embedded in the Spider Queen's crown. I lunged at her and smashed the crown on her head, killing the Spider Queen. I grabbed the Orb of Kindness in an attempt to save Todo with its power, and miraculously, it worked. I revived Todo! Thankfully, Todo accepted the Orb, and after asking his parents for permission, they agreed to let him join our team. We then made our way back to the launch shuttle and departed.

Chapter 4:
My World Just Got Rocked

The gang and I have left Abyss Yonder and are now almost at the Undying Isles, home to Zoltor. We quietly exit the launch shuttle, only to be approached by guards asking to see our passports for entry. Confused, I ask why we need passports, and they explain it's to ensure we are related to Zoltor. I hand over my passport, and they allow my friends and me to enter.

As we step inside, I spot Zoltor's Palace and remember that to find the Forgiving Orb, we must travel through the Zombie Graveyard. Auron, however, tells me he has read all about it and refuses to go through it. I push him slightly, and we start walking.

Suddenly, I step on a branch, and the zombies begin charging at us. In a panic, we fly up into the air after a girl grabs us with her magic broom and lifts us to the top of Mount Doom. She warns us to stay away from the Zombie Graveyard. I explained that I needed the Orb of Forgiveness, but she told me I would never get it because Zoltor guards the orb 24/7. I assert that I am his nephew and will retrieve the Orb. She seems surprised and tells me that all of Zoltor's blood relatives have always turned evil in the end.

I insist I'm not going to be like him and then ask for her name. She replies, "My name is Evelyn." Curious about her flying powers, I ask her how she can fly, and she explains that she's a natural-born witch who has had those abilities since birth.

I tell her I need to get to Zoltor's old family home, but she warns me that his house is actively decaying and urges us to leave before we die. I tell her I'm a risk-taker, so we fly to his old family house. When we arrive, I see that Ana is now in her mid-70s due to the decaying curse.

I tell Evelyn that we need to get the Orb, and we walk into the old family house. I look around, feeling like I've seen this place before, but she insists that I haven't. Then I notice a strange door. I open it and see the Orb of Forgiveness.

As I grab it, an alarm goes off. Turning around, I see Zoltor, who says, "Give me my property, kiddo." I asked him why he turned his family evil. He replies that it wasn't his fault; it was instead the fault of the Grand Council, as well as my mother and father. Hearing that makes my heart sink like a bag of stones. I try to say I'm sorry, but Evelyn grabs me, and we fly back to the launch shuttle.

I sat on the ship, startled and unresponsive, processing everything I had just heard. With the startling realization that my entire bloodline is tainted by the evil of my mother and father, as well as the Grand Council, I begin to question who exactly the Grand Council is.

However, I don't have the luxury of time to ponder that thought as Zoltor suddenly reappears. He seizes our shuttle and smashes it into pieces. I remain still and unmoving while Zoltor engages in a fierce battle with my friends. Then, I step out to save them. Unleashing my demon side, I transform into a black demon and fight Zoltor. After an intense battle, we managed to escape at last.

We arrive at the Ivory Realms, and I'm still trying to understand my uncle's statement. As we enter this golden world, I accidentally step on one of the vines, which grabs me by the leg and slings me around. My friend tries to save me, but the vines ensnare them too.

Just then, a man dressed in gold snaps his fingers, and the vines release us. However, he begins to walk away, and I notice that everything he touches turns to gold. I decide to follow him, but he vanishes, leaving behind a wall of vines that leads us into the dimly lit woods. As we walk down the narrow path, I can't shake off my uncle's words. I wonder why my parents did that to him. I spot a pair of glasses on the ground, pick them up, and put them on. They power on and prompt me to choose one of three secrets. I select the middle option, and a message appears revealing that Zoltor is my uncle, as if I didn't already know that. Just then, the glasses broke. I quickly tell Ana not to put them on.

I see the man in gold again, and this time, I manage to catch up to him. He touches Ana, Auron, Zee-Zee, and Todo, turning them all to gold. I ask who he is, and he replies that he is my grandfather. Confused, I question how that is possible since my grandfather has been dead for years. He explains, "No, I have been here ever since Zoltor, your uncle, locked me away." I ask my grandfather why all of this is happening. He whispers something in my ear that I never expected to hear: "You were not supposed to exist."

When I inquire why, he tells me that the Grand Council created me to start a feud between the Higher Ups and the Lower Downs. I ask him who the Grand Council is, and he explains that they are a celestial group of individuals who thrive on chaos and destruction; without it, they do not exist.

Then I ask why Zoltor locked him away. He replies, "Because my decision in the Council Meeting would have led to Zoltor's being killed on the spot." Next, I inquire about the Higher Ups and the Lower Downs. He tells me that the Higher Ups are the gods of creation, while the Lower Downs are the gods of destruction. There's a plane of existence where a Higher Up and a Lower Down had a child, and that child is me.

I ask my grandfather how to resolve the situation. He tells me that the only way to do so is to stop the Grand Council and their rule over the multiverse before it's too late.

I begin to wonder if Zoltor is even a villain, and my grandfather reassures me, "No, he is your uncle, and he loves you. But the Grand Council must be stopped."

I then ask how to stop them, and he explains that to defeat the Grand Council, I need to collect all the orbs from each realm. With these orbs, I can take their power away. After that, I request him to unfreeze my friends, and he complies. Once he frees them, he disappears, leaving us to venture deeper into the island.

As we explore, I spot the Orb of Empathy, but suddenly, Zoltor appears and snatches it away. I ask to borrow Evelyn's broom, and I start flying after him. Curious, I wondered why he had locked my grandfather away.

He replies that it was because my grandfather would have voted to get rid of me. I press him for more details, but he doesn't answer. Instead, he blasts me off the broom and flies away.

I reflect on my life before all this madness. I remember the day I went to school, walking down the nature path with Auron. We talked about how I was going to his house after school to play video games. Little did I know that would never happen.

Then I wake up and ask my friends to drive us to the Undying Isles to retrieve the Core that Zoltor stole. When we arrive at his palace, I walk right in and demand the Orb from him. He refuses to give it to me, so I pull out a blade and threaten that if he doesn't hand it over, I'll take it by force. He responds, "Bring it on."

Filled with excitement, I attack him, blasting him out of the window. I yell at him, asking why he has to be like this, then slam him to the ground and take the Orb from him. As I do, he says, "You are turning out to be just like me." After that, I walk away and get on the shuttle, where I hand the Orb of Empathy to Ana. She asks why I chose her, and I tell her that she has the most empathy.

Then she leans in and kisses me, which surprises me. Finally, we drive off to the next world, the Ever Isles.

Chapter 5:
Everything Wild

We finally arrive at the Ever Isles, only to find junk scattered everywhere. I spot a flying refrigerator, and Ana sees a hairbrush. When she touches it, the hairbrush grabs her hair and starts to run away with her tangled in it. We chase after the hairbrush, and when we finally catch up, a giant tennis ball starts rolling toward us, so we quickly jump out of the way to avoid being hit.

Suddenly, a jump rope snags Auron, and Zee-Zee gets stuck inside a candy wrapper. The giant tennis ball transforms into a basketball, forcing me to jump into a well to escape. Unfortunately, I find myself trapped with no way out. Evelyn flies down, but her magical powers don't work in this ancient well. I spot a long hallway and tell Evelyn to follow me.

As we walk down the hallway, I open a door and fall onto a card. I quickly jump to the next card, but that one drops down, causing me to fall back into the hallway.

Evelyn manages to jump onto a card and makes it to the other side, so I follow her. However, a card grabs her and pulls her under the clouds. I continue onward in search of the Orb of Generosity.

After exiting the room, I see Evelyn at the end of the hallway and run after her. Suddenly, a magic flying koala grabs me and warns me that if I run any further down the hall, I will become lost in the endless hallway.

He tells me that I don't want to be lost there, as something sinister will get me. I ask him who that is, and he replies that it is the Farewell One, an entity that has haunted this place for years. I inquire if the girl I saw at the end of the hallway is connected to this entity, and the koala confirms that she is.

Just then, the Farewell One starts banging on the door. The koala quickly leads me out of the room, and we reappear in the hallway. I ask him how to escape the well, and he tells me that the only way out is to climb back up, but I must avoid being caught by the Farewell One. I approach the well and begin to climb. As I ascend, I see the Farewell One grabbing the flying koala, and I keep climbing, trying to ignore the blood-curdling scream I hear.

I finally made it out of the well, but none of my friends were there, and the Ever Isles seemed to be cleared of all junk. As the moon rises, I start walking and suddenly see the Farewell One, cloaked in a large black robe, running toward me. In a panic, I fall down a rabbit hole. I finally find Evelyn, and she tells me we need to leave. I ask her why, and she replies that he is always watching. I then ask whom she means, and she tells me it's the Farewell One. Curious, I ask if she has seen his proper form, and she says yes, describing it as hideous. I insist that we need to find the others, and she informs me that they are in the well, along with the koala.

When I ask how she knows all this, she reveals that she has been disguised as the Farewell One. Then, the Farewell One pushes me into the well, and I hit my head and go unconscious. I wake up in a room with all my friends tied to the wall.

I manage to untie myself and my friends, then find the koala. He agrees to help me get the Orb and escape before the Farewell One receives us. He points to a room at the end of the hallway, and we walk in there to find the Orb. However, we see the Farewell One. Eat the koala.

My friend and I tried to get out of there as fast as we could, but then the farewell one grabbed Evelyn. She told us to go on without her and that she would catch up to us. We finally reached the shuttle and waited for five minutes, but Evelyn never came back.

Suddenly, the Farwell One came running at the shuttle, so I started it up, and we took off, seeing Evelyn's ghost outside of the Ever Isles. We all sit in the shuttle, crying at the death of our friend Evelyn. I think to myself, what or who is the farewell one?

We arrive at the Wild Lands, and my team and I are still grappling with the death of Evelyn and the way the Farwell One killed the koala. However, we have to push those thoughts aside.

As we reach a deserted plane station, we notice some safari suits lying on the ground. We pick them up and change into them, then gaze out at the vast expanse of desert that lies ahead. That's when I spotted an older man, probably around 92 years old.

He warns us that if we go past this point, we might not return. I respond that danger awaits us regardless, because I need to collect the Orb of Honesty.

The man informs me that the Orb I seek is on the other side of the expansive desert and jungle. He points us toward a safari jeep, and my friends and I climb in, carefully navigating the vehicle while avoiding potholes on the road.

However, we only make it twenty percent of the way before we run out of gas. By then, it's nighttime, so we exit the jeep and continue on foot. Eventually, we find an oasis and start drinking water, but I pass out from the heat.

When I wake up, it's the next day, and my friends are nowhere in sight. I then see the Grand Council discussing how if Zoltor does not destroy him, they will destroy the entire universe. Returning to reality, I find my friends, and they tell me we need to get through a dense jungle. I ask, "What are we waiting for?"

Suddenly, I see a lion charging at me, so I quickly dodge out of the way. "Let's go around the jungle!" I said. Auron responds that if we go around, we will have to walk across a tightrope bridge. I tell Auron to get moving, and he starts to walk across the bridge.

Out of nowhere, a figure wielding two katanas leaps down, causing Auron to scream in terror. The figure introduces itself in a deep voice as the Death Maker. He draws one of the katanas and slices through one of the ropes on the bridge, prompting another scream from Auron.

I charge at the Death Maker and attempt to fight him. My eyes flash red before returning to their standard color, but then he kicks me, sending me flying off the bridge. I manage to grab onto the edge, barely holding on by a thread. With great effort, I pull myself back up onto the bridge and demand to know why he is following us.

He replies that the League of Darkness has sent him to destroy us. I tell him that I am not one to provoke trouble, and then I kick him off the bridge and continue forward.

We arrive at the ancient ruins and notice two hand slots. Ana and I place our hands in the slots and then walk into the ruins, where snakes and spiders are everywhere, so we have to watch our steps. Suddenly, I step on a trap, and arrows launch at us, prompting us to dodge just in time.

Next, we find ourselves at a podium, and there it is: the Orb of Honesty. I walk up to it, and a voice asks me if I am honest. I reply, "Yes," and suddenly the room turns red. The door behind me and Ana locks, and water starts filling the room. In a moment of panic, I admit, "I'm not honest." The voice asks me why and reminds me that I am the son of Zoltor. It questions why I lied.

I explained that I didn't want everyone to treat me differently. At that moment, the floodwaters stopped. Suddenly, the floor beneath us drops away, and we find ourselves back in the shuttle with the Orb of honesty. Ana suddenly hits me, and I ask, "What was that for?" She replies, "For lying." Then she kisses me, and I ask again, "What was that for?" She responds, "For saving our lives."

Chapter 6:
When Dangerous and Creepy Collide

My friends and I arrive in Hallow Vale, immediately noticing that everyone seems unhappy, sad, and gloomy. However, I spot a girl in a black and white dress with green hair. I approach her and ask what has happened to make everyone feel this way. She explains that long ago, a man named Zoltor took the Orb of Creativity and hid it beyond the Creepy Forest, past the Graves of the Mighty and Powerful, on Mount Unhappiness.

I tell her that I need the Orb to stop Zoltor from ruling over the universe. She informs me that the only way to reach it is by going through the Creepy Forest. I confidently declare that I'm not scared of anything, but Auron admits that he is afraid of trees and dark, scary places. When I ask him why he fears trees, he responds that he thinks they might grab him. I encouraged him to find his courage, and we set off.

As we walk through the Creepy Forest, I suddenly spot a tree with a face. It grabbed Auron by the leg and pulled him down into the mud. I think to myself, "Why does something always go wrong whenever I dive into the mud and find myself in this floating abyss?"

The girl then explains that this place is the realm of future events. I ask her how far into the future the visions can see, and she responds that they can see at least 100 to 200 years ahead.

I look at one of the future events and see myself ruling alongside my father, Zoltor, as the villain, killing my friends. I see Auron at a future ball, where his parents look happy and proud. But as I step beside him, his parents suddenly vanish, and all the decorations from the ball disappear as well.

I pull Auron out of the mud just as I sense Zoltor approaching. He arrives with the Apostles: Copon, Zindin, and Zordin. The Apostles declare that to end this once and for all, they need to drain the child's life energy. However, Zoltor responds that he cannot do that, as it would anger the Grand Council even more.

Coupon informs the Apostles that it doesn't matter if they anger the Grand Council, as the Council has been a thorn in the side of the League of Darkness for millions of years. At that moment, I see Death Maker and The Farewell One arrive. Death Maker speaks to Zoltor, suggesting that if he can capture the entire group, they could be used as sacrifices.

When Zoltor asks, "For what?" Death Maker replies, "For the return of the Ancient Ones." Zoltor counters that they do not need to return. After that, they all leave, and my friends and I continue to the Graves of the Mighty and Powerful.

When we arrive, we walk through silently. However, Auron accidentally steps on a twig, which causes one of the gods to awaken from its eternal sleep and possess Auron. The god tells me that I should have stopped at Peru and warns me that I will die before leaving Auron's body.

I ask Auron to keep moving and not waste any more time, and then we make our way to Mount Unhappiness. As I start walking up the mountain, I feel the weight of my mom's death pressing down on my shoulders, as if I should never have existed.

But I finally made it up to the top and saw the Orb of Creativity. Once I touched it, the Hallow Vale turned into the Happy Vale, with the color returning to the world and everyone being happy. But then I thank the girl for helping me get the Orb of creativity, and I hug her and tell her that I have to go, and then we make our way back to the ship. When we prepare to drive away, I see Death Maker and The Farwell One following after us.

When we arrive at Storm Lake Death Maker, the Farwell One is nowhere to be seen. We find ourselves in a boat when, suddenly, lightning strikes, splitting the ship in half. We swim to shore and spot a fisherman. I ask him what's happening, and he explains that ever since a hole opened in the sky, a storm has been brewing out there, bringing fierce sea creatures, tornadoes, lightning, and even tsunamis that sometimes devastate the village.

As my friends and I walk into town, we notice only three people remaining. I asked one of them what happened to all the residents. He tells me they left after the storm began. Curious, I inquired about the Orb of Responsibility, and he informed me that it was the very thing that caused the storm. To retrieve it, we will need to venture out into the storm.

We suited up in diving gear, ready to retrieve the Orb of Responsibility. As we plunged into the sea, we encountered an electric eel. I drew my sword and attempted to stab the eel, but I was electrocuted in the process.

Ana quickly grabbed me and pulled me along with the rest of the team. We reached the tumultuous waters, bracing ourselves for whatever awaited us in the storm. However, before we could reach our destination, a tornado struck, knocking us underwater.

We managed to crawl back to shore to inform the village that we had failed to stop the storm. The fisherman told us that if we went around to the other side of the storm, there was a back door we could use. He offered to distract the storm from the front along with the remaining villagers while we went through the back door.

We set off on our mission, and my friends and I reached the back door. Just then, I witnessed a massive tsunami obliterating the remaining fishermen.

We entered through the back door, and once we were finally inside, a giant octopus grabbed Ana and Auron and pulled them underwater. I had to dive in to try to save them. While I was down there, I spotted the Orb of Responsibility, but I decided to leave it alone and focus on rescuing my friends first.

Finally, I found my friends, but the octopus was trying to eat them. I quickly took my harpoon and stabbed the octopus in the eye, then pulled my friends to safety. We made our way into the water room, where the Orb of Responsibility was located. As I approached it, the glass surrounding the Orb began to crack.

I leaped for the Orb and ended up supported by only one piece of glass. I asked Ana to take the Orb and return it to the top of the mountain to stop the storm. She started walking up the hill and carefully placed the Orb in its designated spot. As she did, the storm ceased, and the water calmed down. I flew out of the water but realized I had lost my second life and now only had one left. I told them that I didn't need to die for a third time.

Ana then asked me when it was the first time I passed away. I explained that it happened in the water caves in Peru on the way to the launch shuttle. Instead of responding, she hugged me tightly and told me to be careful. I reassured her that I was going to be fine.

As we made our way back to the village, we saw that the fishermen had returned. I asked them how they managed to survive, and they told me that they had swum back to shore. I promised them that I would bring the rest of the fishing people back safely. They expressed their gratitude, and then we headed towards the shuttle.

We arrive in the peaceful vale, and everything seems perfectly in order. No one speaks a word, but then I spot someone and ask why it is so quiet here. She tells me it's because the Farewell One and the Death Maker are forcing everyone to search for information about the Ancient Ones.

I question why they are doing this and suggest that if they don't want to, they shouldn't have to obey those rules. I then ask her what the Ancient Ones are. She explains that they were great bounty hunters and challengers with the power to shake the Earth. I inquire about how to bring them back, but she admits she doesn't know the way.

I reassure her that as long as no one knows how to resurrect them, we will be fine. Next, I ask her where to find the Orb of Loyalty. She starts searching through files to locate it and finally informs me that it's not on this island.

Curious, I ask her where to find it, and she reveals that it is on the island next to this one. She explains that the only way to reach that island is by using a magic boat. I ask her where that boat is, and she replies that it lies beneath the Forgotten Sea. I then ask her to take us there, but just as we arrive, the Farewell One catches up to us.

Ana and I engage in a fight with the Farewell One while the others dive into the ocean to fetch the boat. However, the Farewell One proves to be too strong, and we are defeated. We have no choice but to dive into the ocean to assist our friends in retrieving the ship so we can travel to the other island. Now that we have the flying boat, we can make it to the other island.

The ship ascends into the sky, and Ana and I begin discussing what will happen after we stop Zoltor. I explained to her that Zoltor isn't the real problem; it's the Grand Council that we need to stop. She asks me what I mean, and I tell her that we must stop the Grand Council before Zoltor can find the Orb of Balance.

She inquires about how we will find the Orb of Balance, and I explain that we need to collect all 14 orbs and merge them to create the Orb of Balance. She agrees, stating that we will stop the Grand Council, to which I respond, "Yes."

We then arrive at the island, where we see the Orb of Loyalty. Just as I reach for it, the Grand Council appears and tells me to stop or face the consequences. I assert that they are the real problem, and then they use their powers to conjure weapons. I say to my friends that if we want the Orb, we must confront them. My friends agree, saying, "Gladly," and we engage in battle with the Grand Council.

During the fight, I managed to grab the Orb, but then the head of the Grand Council used his dark magic to pull both of us into an empty void. He demanded that I give him the Orb. In response, I activated my power and returned to reality.

As I charged up, they saw a fiery red version of me that they had never encountered before, and then they fled. Now that we have the Orb of Loyalty, we're ready to leave, but then the girl we met earlier asks if she can join us to escape this place. Tormented, I ask her name, and she says her name is Coco. I tell her to come on, and then I give her the Orb of Loyalty.

We board the ship and leave the Peaceful Vale. We arrive at the Onyx Mines, where everything is made of charcoal, and little trolls are busy mining. I accidentally bump into one of the trolls, who introduces himself as Ivan. Curious, I ask him why everyone is mining and what they are searching for. He explains that the Miner has instructed them to work until they reach their Ever Point. I inquire about the Ever Point, and he tells me it is the moment they find their Gemstone, which will take them to Heaven.

I turn to Ana and say that each world we visit seems to get weirder, and she agrees. I then tell Ivan that he doesn't have to keep mining. When he asks why, I explain that he doesn't need a gem to get into Heaven. I ask him how long the Miner has had control over this place, and he replies that it has been ever since a hole opened in the sky, allowing the Miner to arrive.

I shared with him that a similar hole opened in my world, which caused many of my friends' parents to disappear. Ever since then, I have been trying to fix this situation. Ivan asks if he can help resolve this madness, and I respond with a yes. I promise that once everything is set right, I will bring him back to his home realm. He thanks me for this.

Next, I ask Ivan where I can find the Orb of Courage. He tells me that the Miner guards it, but he also mentions that a group of people in gold robes once gave him the Orb. I mean that the Grand Council created the Orbs.

I then ask Ivan how we can reach the Miner. He explains that we must go through the Caves of Despair before we can get to his Earth Castle. I request that Ivan take me to the Caves of Despair, and we begin making our way there.

As we approach, I see the rock monsters waiting for us. I walk up to them, and they charge at me. Suddenly, I noticed an iron glove made of rocks. I put it on and punched the rock monsters, causing them to fall apart.

We continue through the caves until we reach a lava drop-off with three bridges. If we choose the wrong one, we risk falling into our doom. I take a chance and walk across the first bridge, but it turns out to be the wrong path. I have to jump to the next bridge, which is the correct one, and we all make it across.

Just then, the Death Maker appears and attacks us. I ask him why the League of Darkness sent him after us, and he replies, "Because they want you dead, and it will please the Grand Council." I tell him that he isn't going to kill me. Then he pulls out two katanas and starts fighting me. I forge two katanas of my own and stab him, causing him to fall off the bridge. However, I see him crawl back up and walk away.

We finally reached the entrance of the Miners' Castle. As we quietly walked in, I spotted the Orb of Loyalty in one of the rooms. I grabbed it, but an alarm suddenly went off. I asked Ivan where the Miner was, and he replied that he didn't know.

We walked out of the front doors of the castle, and I announced to everyone that they were free from the Miners' rule. Suddenly, the Miners' Castle flew up into the air and left the Onyx Mines.

We made our way to our ship and discussed where the Miner might have gone. That's when I saw Death Maker jump into the ocean and swim away, but I chose not to pay it any attention. We left the Onyx Mines, and shortly after, the mines exploded. I told Ivan about the explosion, and he began to cry. I then turned to Ana and said that the Grand Council had gone too far and that we needed to gather the Orbs quickly.

Chapter 7:
The Perfect Moon

We arrive at the Immortal Moon, a place shrouded in darkness and danger, resembling a scene from a horror book. As we start walking, an alarm suddenly goes off, and the gravity turns off, sending us floating 12 feet into the air. Then, just as abruptly, it stops, and we crash back to the ground. We get back up and begin asking people if they know where to find the Orb of Patience.

I soon realize that I'm not talking to humans; I'm conversing with werewolves and vampires. Ana, Auron, Todo, and Carlos become scared and run off to a creepy haunted house. They open the door, but a ghost grabs them, and the door slams shut behind them.

Determined to save our friends, Zee-Zee, Coco, and I rush into the house. We notice a spiral staircase that seems to stretch infinitely upward, but we can't see any sign of our friends. As we start walking up the stairs, I spot the ghost that took our friends. I grab its tail and fly up the stairs with it attached to the back of me.

Then I see Ana, and I let go of the ghost. Suddenly, I leave reality and find myself among the Grand Council and the Five Demonic Spirits, who are discussing something. The Grand Council removes their robes, revealing themselves as the Ancient Ones. Then, I return to reality, grab Ana, hug her tightly, and ask if she remembers when we overheard the Five Demonic Spirits talking about the Ancient Ones. She says yes, and I inform her that the Ancient Ones are the Grand Council. She looks surprised.

I tell her that we need to find the rest of our friends, and she mentions that she saw them further up the stairs. I fly up and spot Auron, so I grab him. Next, I see Carlos and hold onto him as well. Then, I find Todo and catch him, too. After that, I spot Zee-Zee and Coco and grab them as well. Together, we fly out of the haunted house, and I tell them that I know where the Orb of Patience is located. They ask where, and I inform them that it is in the Eternal Moon Castle.

We make our way to the Eternal Moon Castle, and when we arrive, I kick the door open. Inside, I see the Orb, but I also spot Zoltor. I call out to him, "Uncle!" He responds, "What?" as I walk up to him and hug him. Confused, he asks, "What is this?" I explain that I know the Grand Council is evil.

He questions how I found this out, and I tell him that I had a vision where I saw them talking. I explain that the only way to stop them is to use the Orbs to create the Orb of Balance. I then ask if I can have the Orb of Generosity, and he hands it to me. I inquire if he is joining us, and he replies that he is.

And then I grab the Orb of Patience, and then we go back to the ship, and we prepare to leave, and then I see Death Maker and The Farwell One staring at us as we leave.

We finally arrive at the Perfect Nation, a place free from violence. The military greets us warmly and escorts us to the Moonlit Hotel for our stay. After checking in, we met an army sergeant named Apo, who asked if we needed anything. We assure him we're fine, and he walks away.

We decide to head down to the pool to relax, but Ana expresses her concern about something feeling off about the island. She mentions that there are arguments and disagreements everywhere. I reassure her that everything is fine and suggest we not dwell on it.

While I continue to the Volcanic Bay, Ana chooses to stay at the hotel with Zoltor to chat. Suddenly, the army sergeant reappears and attacks Zoltor, revealing himself to be one of the Five Demonic Spirits. He attempts to kill Ana, but she skillfully fights back and kicks him out of the window. When she looks down, he has vanished.

Determined to find our friends, Ana, Zoltor set out on a search. However, upon arriving at Volcanic Bay, they discover that their friends are no longer there. Suddenly, the Grand Council and the Five Demonic Spirits appear and capture Zoltor and Ana. Auron and I witness this unfold and rush to save them. While we manage to rescue Zoltor, Ana is taken away, disappearing before our eyes.

In a desperate move, I grab hold of a member of the Grand Council before they vanish, inadvertently saving Ana in the process. Enraged, the Grand Council exclaims that this was never part of their plan.

I respond, "What do you mean?" They explain, "This whole event was intended to create a disruption, allowing the Ancient Ones to return finally." When I ask why they want them back, they reply that it is to unleash absolute chaos and destruction. I tell them that this is wrong, but they didn't listen and left.

Then, the Perfect Nation begins to fall apart. I spot the Orb of Self-Awareness and run to grab it, dodging falling bricks and trees. I manage to obtain it and make it back to the shuttle, barely escaping. Just then, I hear my mom calling out to me; she tells me that the Grand Council and Zoltor need to be stopped. I respond that Zoltor is the victim here, and then I turn to leave. I get in the shuttle and tell Zoltor that if he pulls a stunt that will mess up the entire mission, it will not be suitable for him. He says yes, and then the shuttle drives off.

Chapter 8:
Running Away from The Clock

The gang and I arrive at one of the final realms to collect the last two Orbs. We enter the Love Valley and Ana and I exchange glances as we take in the giant heart-shaped building and a broken fountain that holds the Orb of Positive Attitude. When we try to grab it, however, it won't budge. We notice a letter stating that if we want the Orb, we must complete five love-bonding tasks.

As we read this, five different buildings light up, and one of them beckons me forward. The first building that lights up is labeled "Friendship," so Auron and I walk inside. To our surprise, Auron sees his parents there, and I start telling them about the dangers we're facing. They express their intention to leave this planet when the dangers arise. Auron then looks at me with hurt in his eyes and accuses me of being the reason his parents are gone, claiming that I knew this was going to happen from day one.

I apologize, but he walks away, leaving me feeling sad and as if the world has turned against me. I muster the courage to approach him again and ask how I can make things right. He responds that the only way to fix it is to bring his parents back. I assure him that if we can stop the Grand Council, I will be able to restore his parents. I hug him tightly, and he asks me if I promise. I nod and say yes, promising that I will do everything I can.

As we walk out of the building together, Auron finally tells me, "I forgive you." At that moment, one of the rings on the fountain lights up, signaling our progress.

The next building illuminates, labeled "Perusian Friend," and I enter the room with Carlos. Inside, a painful memory plays: I had once told him that I could restore everything, but now I see the desolate state of Peru.

I try to explain that it wasn't my fault, but Carlos yells that it is all my fault. He insists that if I had never been born, none of this would have ever happened. I assure him that once we defeat the Council, we will restore Peru to its natural glory. We then hug and walk out of the building. After a moment, he tells me, "I forgive you," and then another ring on the fountain lights up.

The next room lights up with the label "First Love." Ana and I enter, and she asks me if I have ever liked her. I tell her that I have had feelings for her since the fifth grade, and that feeling has never changed. Then she asked me if I wanted to be her boyfriend, and I said yes. She grabs me and kisses me, causing my face to turn red. After that, we walk out of the room, and another ring on the fountain lights up, signaling the next room: "Family Chaos."

My uncle Zoltor and I walk in together. I asked him why he caused this mess in the first place. He explains that the Council, along with my mother and father, would have never accepted me. I then asked him, "If the council made me a docent, does that mean they are my parents?" He responds that, in a way, they are. After that, I hug him, and we walk out of the room. I tell him I forgive him.

Just then, the last Ringo on the fountain lights up, and the Orb falls to the ground. I pick it up and announce to everyone that we now only have one more Orb to collect before we can stop the Grand Council. Then we head to the shuttle to go to the last world.

We arrive at the final destination, the Faint Sanctuary. As we step out of the shuttle, we notice churches and nuns everywhere, but we quickly shift our focus to finding the Orb. Suddenly, the sky turns a dark red, prompting us to work even harder.

We approach one of the nuns to ask about the Orb of Humility. She informs us that she knows where it is located, so we follow her into the church. Once inside, I ask the pastor if he knows the Orb's whereabouts. He tells us that the Orb is on Mt. Religious, and I request that he guide us up the mountain.

As we begin our ascent, the sky turns an ominous shade of red. Ana and I discuss the urgency of retrieving the Orb, emphasizing that if we don't act soon, the Ancient Ones will return. I urge the pastor to hurry, explaining that we have someone important to be. He replies that patience is a virtue, but I insist that I don't have time to waste.

Eventually, I spot the Orb of Humility, but it's encased within a tombstone. I've heard that those who enter never return. Auron then tells me that I have nothing to lose. He throws me the Orb, closes the tomb, and says, "You were my best friend." Tragically, the tomb then kills him. I sit there in tears, but Ana grabs me and insists that we have to go. I agree with her, and as we leave, I swear that I will get my revenge.

Chapter 9:
When Times Are on Their Side

We sit in the ship, grappling with the reality of our friend Auron's recent death. We know we need to stop the Grand Council from taking what little remains of our world. In the back of the ship, Ana and I discuss what might happen once we defeat the Grand Council. I emphasize that the key word in that sentence is "if" we defeat them.

Ana asks me what I mean by that, and I explain that if my power isn't strong enough, I won't be able to stop them. My friends reassure me that I don't have to face this challenge alone, but I respond that I don't want anyone else to die because of me.

Zoltor then interjects, saying that the Grand Council knows everyone's moves before they make them. This battle feels like a game of chess. I ask him how we can defeat them, and he tells me that to beat them while they are playing chess, we need to be playing checkers.

I ask him how we do that, and he explains that if we want any chance of winning, we need to go to the Forge to merge the Orbs and create the Orb of Balance. After that, we should go to the Weapons Hall to acquire the right weapons.

I look around at everyone and say, "This journey is for the koala, Evelyn, Auron, my mother, and father, as well as for every other human and animal that has died." They all nod in agreement, and we begin our journey to the Forged Realm.

When we arrive, we find the place in complete chaos. Suddenly, I see orbs falling from the sky, shattering upon impact, and revealing hollow figures dressed in golden robes. These figures begin to attack the people of the Forged Lands, so we fight back against them. Amid the battle, one of the figures grabs Zee-Zee and Coco, and then they vanish.

After defeating the remaining figures, we request an audience with the Forger, who directs us up the hill to his home. As we rush up the mountain, an earthquake suddenly strikes, separating the Forged Lands and leaving Ana and me on one side while Carlos ends up on the other. We continue running up the hill until we finally see the Forger.

I ask him if he can help us, and he inquires about our needs. I explain that we need him to forge the fourteen orbs. He responds that he requires his forging tools, which were taken by one of the golden-robed figures. Ana and I spot the figure who has his tools, and we confront him, fighting to retrieve them. After a struggle, we manage to reclaim the tools and return to the Forger.

I handed him his tools and the fourteen orbs, and he began the forging process. Soon after, the Grand Council arrived, leading to a confrontation with us. In the heat of the moment, I threw a dagger at them, but they managed to catch it. Zoltor and Ana then engaged in a fight with the Council while I waited for the forger to finish making the Orb of Balance. Unfortunately, Zoltor and Ana were defeated, and the Grand Council started walking toward me.

At that moment, the forger completed the Orb of Balance. I held it out toward them, but they grabbed it and smashed it with their bare hands. They then seized me by the throat, called me useless, and threw me into the ocean. Zoltor dove in after me to save me, while the Grand Council took Carlos and Ana away.

Once Zoltor rescued me and brought me back to the ship, I asked him where Ana and Carlos were. He explained that the Grand Council had taken them. Overcome with emotion, I began to cry, feeling the weight of losing all my friends. I asked Zoltor what the point was in going on without them, and he urged me to focus on saving my friends.

I then asked him how we were going to defeat the Grand Council. He told me there was still a chance: if we could make it to the Hall of Weapons, we could obtain the right kind of weapons to defeat the Grand Council. I insisted that he drive us there, so we set off towards the Hall of Weapons.

When we arrived, we discovered that someone was already inside. As we walked in, we confronted The Farwell One, Death Maker, and The Miner. They charged at us, and in that moment, my uncle stepped in to protect me. Unfortunately, he couldn't stop them, and The Farwell One grabbed him, taking him onto their ship, leaving me all alone.

Just then, I heard a scream coming from down the hall. I ran to open the door and found my dad. I saved Jeremy, who looked at me and asked, "Jacob, is that you?" I replied, "Yes," and we hugged tightly.

I asked my dad for help to stop them, and he said we needed the whole family to join us, along with the weapons in the hall. So, my dad and I gathered all the weapons we could find, boarded the ship, and prepared to rescue Grandpa from the Ivory Realms.

When we arrived at the Ivory Realms, I saw Grandpa, shimmering like gold as he always had been. I asked him how we could free him, and he told us that my dad and I needed to use our combined power to set him free. We succeeded, and he returned to his usual self. We urged him to come with us.

I turned to my dad and asked if Mom was alive. He confirmed that she was and told me she was in the Unassigned Lands. We traveled there and found her. When we asked for her help, she agreed. As soon as she saw Dad, they embraced for the first time in a long time.

Then I wondered, "Grandpa, where is Grandma?" He replied that she had passed away some time ago. I expressed my condolences, saying, "I'm sorry for your loss." After that, I reminded everyone that we still needed to save Zoltor.

Then my dad asks me why we need to save Zoltor, and I reply, "Because he is family." After that, we make our way to The Grand Planet, where we see the Grand Council's palace. We land the ship, then the boat, and enter the palace. Once inside, we find that they have Zoltor. My dad saves him, and they share a hug. Zoltor apologizes to his brother.

I then remind them that we need to save my friends. I search for the room where they are being held, and when I find them, I free them. Ana runs towards me and kisses me, and I tell her I love her. I explain that we need to stop the Grand Council, so I hand out weapons to everyone.

Finally, we walk into the main room where the Grand Council is gathered. In a moment of desperation, I stab one of the council members in the stomach, and they drop their coats. To my shock, they are revealed to be the Ancient Ones.

They grab me by the throat and throw me out of the window. The main one flies out after me, and we engage in a fierce fight. I hear Zoltor scream as his lifeless body falls from the window, and in my anguish, I cry and scream.

Driven by both rage and determination, I use my weapon to behead the main council member. In that moment, I leave reality and witness the future unfold before me. When I return to reality, I gather my strength and eliminate the remaining council members. Afterwards, I pass out.

When I wake up, I find everyone gathered around me. I hug my mom and dad tightly and express my gratitude to everyone. We then return to the Peaceful Nation and begin to settle into our new lives. Five years pass, and we adapt to our new surroundings, unaware of the danger that awaits us in the years to come.

The End